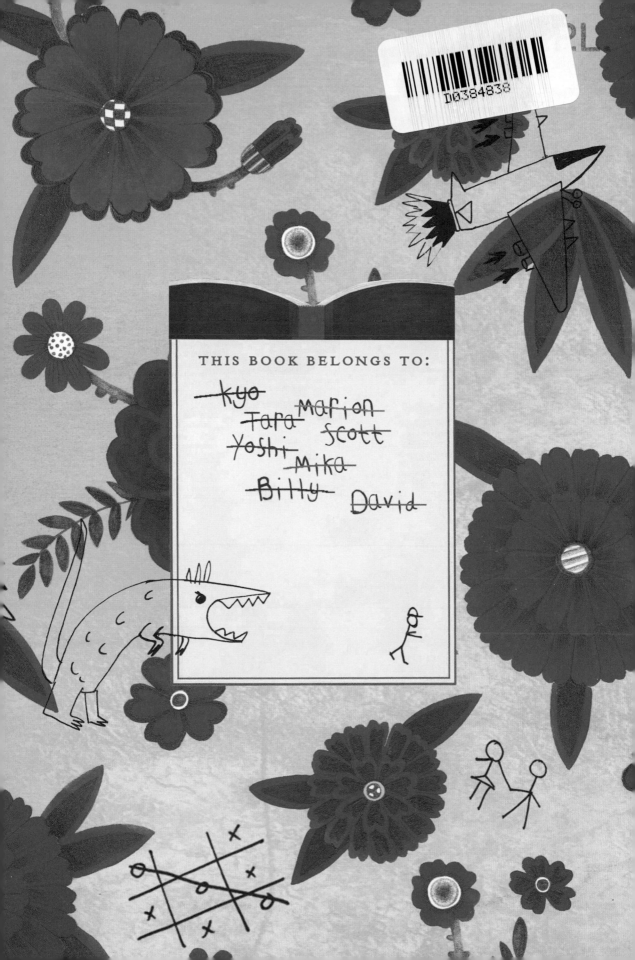

THE
GOOD
LITTLE
BOOK

WORDS BY **KYO MACLEAR**

PICTURES BY **MARION ARBONA**

TUNDRA BOOKS

For my booky boys: David, Yoshi and Mika
With thanks to the best book club ever: Tara, Marion and Scott
K. M.

To Billy, without whom I would be nothing
M. A.

TEXT COPYRIGHT © 2015 BY KYO MACLEAR
ILLUSTRATIONS COPYRIGHT © 2015 BY MARION ARBONA

Published in Canada and the United States of America by Tundra Books,
a division of Random House of Canada Limited, a Penguin Random House Company

Library of Congress Control Number: 2014951821

LIBRARY AND ARCHIVES CANADA CATALOGUING IN PUBLICATION

Maclear, Kyo, 1970-, author
The good little book / by Kyo Maclear ; illustrated by Marion Arbona.

Issued in print and electronic formats.
ISBN 978-1-77049-451-0 (bound).—ISBN 978-1-77049-452-7 (epub)

I. Arbona, Marion, 1982-, illustrator II. Title.

PS8625.L435G66 2015   jC813'.6   C2014-906426-8
                                                C2014 906427-6

Edited by Tara Walker | Designed by CS Richardson
The artwork in this book was rendered in gouache and pencil.
The text was set in Tribute.

www.tundrabooks.com
www.penguinrandomhouse.ca

Printed and bound in China

1 2 3 4 5 6   20 19 18 17 16 15

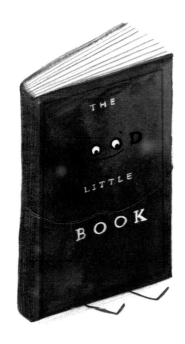

Outside of a dog, a book is a man's best friend.
Inside of a dog it's too dark to read.

GROUCHO MARX

ONCE THERE WAS A GOOD LITTLE BOOK. It had fine
printed pages and a simple cover and a strong spine. It sat on a
shelf in a study lined with other books. There were thick books
and thin books. Books for racing through quickly and books for
savoring slowly.

Some books were popular.

Others were less popular.

The good little book was neither thick nor thin,
popular nor unpopular. It had no shiny
medals to boast of. It didn't even own
a proper jacket.

One day a boy drifted into the study. This boy had
just landed himself in trouble and had been sent off to
"think things over." Which is what he did for exactly
twelve seconds. Then he began to explore.

Seeing that the room was full of ancient stuff that didn't do anything, the boy pulled out the good little book. And with a great sigh, he began to read.

The silence of reading slowly filled the room. It spread through the walls and ceilings and spilled into the street.

The wind whistled through
a crack in the window. The
clock ticked in the corner.
But the boy didn't notice.

The book the boy thought couldn't do anything
did many things. It carried him to the deep sea
and steered him towards a faraway land.

It dazzled him and stumped him and made
him laugh and gasp. He read it through. Then he
turned back to the beginning and read it again.

Winter came and snow fell on the city. No matter what his days held in store, the boy never tired of reading the good little book. It didn't turn him into a bookish boy, or improve his naughty behavior, but it did become a loyal companion, there to see him to sleep and distract him when he had to "think things over."

Spring came and rain fell on the city. The good little book continued to accompany the boy everywhere. Until, one day, something terrible happened . . .

The boy lost his favorite book.

He retraced his steps, searching and
searching, hunting for hours . . .
but the good little book was gone.

In his distress, he pictured the worst.

Fires and Floods.

Bandits and Bears.

The boy worried. How would such a good and quiet book
survive? What would it do if it found itself at the edge of
the unknown? Or among frightful enemies?

You see, the good little book did not have skills that would
help it in the dangerous wild or in the rushing streets. It
wasn't even wearing a proper jacket.

If only it were a *sensible* book of languages
or a *useful* book of information.

If only it were loud enough to make itself noticeable.

The boy sought help but discovered that very few people have time for a lost book — no matter how good or little it might be.

He put up posters.

He went to places books like to go.

Until, finally, he ended up at the library.

But his book was not there either.

Summer came and petals and pollen fell on the city. As the
boy waited for the book to turn up, he began to read other
books to pass the time. He space-traveled, time-traveled and
elephant-traveled all over the world and beyond.

At first it made little difference. No matter how many nearly
good books he read, the boy still felt that the good little book
had been written especially for him.

But slowly his heart began to open to other stories.

Little did he know that his lost book had been noticed.
The animals had noticed.

A squirrel thought it might be a thriller.

A sparrow thought it might
be a romance.

A raccoon thought it
might be a sandwich.

A cat sat on it to keep it warm.

And a little girl had noticed too.

Autumn came and leaves fell on the city. The boy was out one morning when something caught his eye.

He stopped and opened his mouth to say something.
Then he closed his mouth and let the girl and the book go.

But it didn't really go.

You see, a good little book never completely goes away.

In the seasons that followed, the book the
boy thought too quiet and helpless to
survive in the world did just fine.

In fact, you could even say it blossomed.